AWFUL THE MANY FOUL DEEDS

DAVID BRETT SAUNDERS

Books by David Brett Saunders

ROMANS & BRITONS
For Honour And Not For Glory

VIKINGS & SAXONS
All Sins Must Be Paid For

LATER MIDDLE AGES
Cast No Shadow

HIGH MIDDLE AGES
Awful The Many Foul Deeds

Copyright © 2021 David Brett Saunders

Designed by Jeremy Paxton

Set in 11pt Palatino Linotype

Printed in the UK

All rights reserved

1 4 6 8 10 12 14 16 18

ISBN: 978-0-9567753-7-5

List of Contents

*Still being dedicated to my
wife Bev and my daughters
Emma, Claire and Amy*

*Also dedicated to the memory of the marvellous
Channel 4 archaeological dig TV series Time Team*

*And still in continued fond remembrance of
all the wonderful books of Rosemary Sutcliff*

A Literary Quote

"Ah! Vanitas Vanitatum!
Which of us is happy in this world?
Which of us has his desire?
Or, having it, is satisfied? -
Come, children, let us shut up the box
and the puppets,
For our play is played out"

ending of 1848 published novel Vanity Fair
by William Makepeace Thackeray (1811-1863)

List of Fictional Characters

RORY
Formerly called Ruaidri, orphan boy taken in by Lady Affreca

EVA
Formerly called Aoife, his younger sister also taken in as well

BROGAN
An old harper who helps to teach Rory

DAVID LE GRISHOMME
Man-at-arms for Prince Arthur and others

NIGEL DE MALPAS
Villainous man-at-arms in employ of King John

MCGUINN and MCGUIRE
Cut-throats and thieves

List of Historical Characters

HENRY II (CURTMANTLE)
King of England 1154 – 1189; born in 1133

RICHARD I (LIONHEART)
King of England 1189 – 1199; born in 1157

JOHN I (LACKLAND)
King of England 1199 – 1216; born in 1166

DIARMAIT MAC MURCHADA
King of Leinster; lived c.1110 – 1171

RUAIDRI UA CONCHOBAIR
Last High King of Ireland; lived c.1116 – 1198

LLYWELYN FAWR (THE GREAT)
Prince of Gwynedd; lived c.1173 – 1240

MADOG AP GRUFFUDD
Prince of Powys Fadog from 1191 to 1236

GWENWYNWYN AP OWAIN
Prince of Powys Wenwynwyn; died 1216

RICHARD DE CLARE (STRONGBOW)
Earl of Pembroke; lived 1130 – 1176

WILLIAM DE BRAOSE
4th Lord of Bramber; lived c.1144/1153 – 1211

MAUD DE BRAOSE
Wife of William after 1166; lived c.1155 – 1210

JOHN DE COURCY
Became ruler of much of Ulster; lived 1150 – 1219

AFFRECA DE COURCY
Daughter of Godred Olafsson; died c.1219

GODRED OLAFSSON
Ruler of the Kingdom of the Isles; died 1187

RAGNVALD GODREDSSON
Brother of Affreca and later King of the Isles; died 1229

HUGH DE LACY
Became 1st Earl of Ulster; lived c.1176 – 1242

PRINCE ARTHUR
Duke of Brittany; born 1187; disappeared c.1203

Statement

As surely as the sun rises so man is born to conflict, and the lands of Ireland and Wales have been subject to more than their fair share of troubles from incursions by their bigger and incessantly meddlesome neighbour England ......

Historical Introduction – 1166 to 1175

In the 12th Century whilst in the reign of the English King Henry II, the kings of different provinces of Ireland were often fighting amongst themselves for territory and overall supremacy.

Following the killing of the previous High King Muirchertach Mac Lochlainn in 1166, the powerful King of Connacht Ruaidri Ua Conchobair rode to Dublin and was installed as the new High King of Ireland, arguably the first for some time without too much opposition.

One of Ruaidri's first acts was to invade Leinster with the men of Connacht and the help of the Dubliners and to depose his great enemy and its King, Diarmait Mac Murchada, and expel him from the lands of Ireland.

Mac Murchada fled to Wales in 1167 and thence to England to seek the support of King Henry II in the recruitment of soldiers to help reclaim his kingship, and thereby set into motion a chain of events that changed the course of Irish history forever.

King Henry was reluctant to help and get involved in an expensive war, but he had been given permission by the Pope some time before to claim Ireland as part of his kingdom in order to help reform the Church over there.

So he gave Mac Murchada permission to privately recruit anyone he could from amongst the English barons, lords and knights prepared to aid him.

Diarmait Mac Murchada went to Bristol in the South West of England and was able to enlist as mercenaries some strong and significant lords and their fighting men.

Many of these Anglo-Norman barons came from the Welsh Marches border regions and were ripe to be persuaded to leave the bitter fighting in Wales to head over to seek their fame and fortune in Ireland.

These men included the Earl of Pembroke Richard FitzGilbert, Robert FitzStephen and Maurice and Raymond FitzGerald.

Richard FitzGilbert also called Richard de Clare was better known to his friends and enemies by the nickname of Strongbow, and he had fallen out with King Henry in the past and so was looking for opportunities elsewhere.

A venture in Ireland seemed to fit the bill and furthermore if successful Mac Murchada had even promised his own daughter Aoife in marriage and also the possibility of becoming King of Leinster on his death.

Finally in May 1169 some of the barons landed in South East Ireland with hundreds of soldiers, archers and cavalry and swiftly recruited another five hundred Irishmen loyal to Mac Murchada to swell their numbers.

They laid siege to the Norse-Irish town of Wexford and forced it to submit once again to Diarmait Mac Murchada, who then promptly gave Wexford and its surrounding area to these lesser barons as payment.

Temporarily a peace treaty was signed, granting Mac Murchada rights and recognising Ua Conchobair as the High King, and hostages were given and taken.

But in 1170 there were further Anglo-Norman landings led by Strongbow, the Earl of Pembroke, and the invaders quickly seized Waterford and Dublin and fully restored Mac Murchada as the King of Leinster.

As promised Strongbow married Diarmait's fair daughter Aoife to give strength to the alliance and also continue the protection being given by the Anglo-Norman barons.

Then Diarmait Mac Murchada died in May 1171 and Strongbow felt empowered to claim the kingship of Leinster.

The High King of Ireland, Ruaidri Ua Conchobair, now united the Irish forces and with his large army instigated a campaign to retake the lands lost to the Anglo-Norman raiders.

They regained some territory and laid siege to Dublin, but Strongbow turned the tables by sallying out early one morning and attacking the unprepared Irish and defeating them most soundly. Ua Conchobair retired humiliated back to Connacht, now High King in name only.

At this point King Henry II suddenly took more notice. When word got back that the man he knew as the Earl of Pembroke had established himself as the king of a province of Ireland he was furious.

He had only meant to give permission for his countrymen to help Mac Murchada militarily, not to contest his power and rival his own authority.

King Henry cut off supplies from England and organised an expedition to Ireland himself with a large army arriving in Waterford in October 1171.

Realising that the king could and would defeat him, Strongbow intercepted King Henry and offered his apologies and begged forgiveness.

King Henry II allowed Strongbow to remain now as the Lord of Leinster and also took the homage as their overlord of most of the Irish kings; who initially saw him not as an imperial conqueror but more as their protector against potential further expansionism by Strongbow and the other Anglo-Norman barons.

Then at the Synod of Cashel in 1172 the bishops of Ireland assembled at the Cathedral on the Rock of Cashel and agreed to a number of reforms to bring the Irish Church into line with the Roman Church under the leadership of the Pope.

Also just before King Henry returned to England in April 1172 he ordered set aside Dublin which was no longer to be part of Leinster but rather to be owned by the king himself.

And the province of Meath, which had already been invaded by Strongbow's men, was instead given as a lordship to the older Hugh de Lacy, a loyal supporter of the king, which must have angered Strongbow somewhat as well.

Finally later on in 1175 certain issues were supposed to be resolved by the Treaty of Windsor, which acknowledged King Henry as overlord of all conquered territory but also recognised Ruaidri Ua Conchobair as High King of all lands outside conquered Meath and Leinster.

However the adherence to the provisions of the Treaty soon fell apart on both sides, especially as King Henry's attentions were drawn away to deal with a revolt against him by his sons and wife.

The Anglo-Norman lords continued to increase their power and enlarge their lands and they also started to build castles – firstly just with earthen motte and wooden bailey walls; then in due course came more formidable stone castles.

Competing rivalries led to the growing suppression of the ordinary people of Ireland and an extensive process of colonisation took place along with the imposition of a feudal system.

Prologue – 1176 to 1197

When Strongbow died in May 1176 the lordship of Leinster passed back into the hands of King Henry, who later granted all his rights as Lord of Ireland to his youngest son Prince John, who ever after showed little respect towards the people of Ireland.

And in a marked change of policy towards Ireland, King Henry II now encouraged the Anglo-Norman barons to actually extend their activities and conquer more territory.

A young and ambitious Anglo-Norman knight of noble birth but bleak prospects, John de Courcy fought his way to the notice of King Henry who laughingly granted him rights to the lands of Ulster "provided he could conquer it by force".

Early in January 1177 John de Courcy assembled a small army of twenty-two knights and about three hundred foot soldiers and marched North from Dublin at a fast pace of roughly thirty miles a day aiming to gain control of the province of Ulaid.

They skirted round the back of the Mourne Mountains and took the town of Downpatrick in East Ulster by surprise and captured it.

Then following several fierce battles through February to June 1177 the bold de Courcy and his disciplined troops managed to defeat the last King of Ulaid, Rory Mac Dunlevy.

After conquering most of Eastern Ulster, John established his main base at Carrickfergus where he proceeded to build a large and impressive stone castle.

Around 1180 he married Affreca, the daughter of Godred Olafsson, the Norseman who ruled the Kingdom of the Isles – basically incorporating the Isle of Man, the Hebrides Isles and other islands in the Firth of Clyde.

This was most probably a convenient arranged marriage that sealed a mutually beneficial alliance of security and support. However John and Affreca were married for many years and appeared devoted and both were pious and later endowed several religious establishments.

Subsequently John de Courcy also built another strong stone castle at Dundrum to control access into the region from the West and South, standing tall on top of a rocky hill commanding fine views South over Dundrum Bay and the Mourne Mountains.

Thus over time de Courcy proceeded to build up a great power base in Eastern Ulster, and had proved so successful that he incurred the displeasure of both King Henry II and also later on his son who had become King Richard I.

He was a bold and immensely strong warrior with a reputation to be feared, but who was also well respected by many of the local Irish population.

John de Courcy erected castles, built bridges and repaired churches and generally governed the province relatively peacefully to the better benefit of its inhabitants.

He wielded massive power for many, many years and was able to defy all these different kings – until the days of King John's accession to the throne and the start of future conflict.

PART ONE
1198 – 1205

Chapter 1 – 1198

There had always been feuding between the different Irish clans and the recent death of the last High King of Ireland, Ruaidri Ua Conchobair, had increased tensions and led to more recent raids in and around Ulster.

The latest attack had burned down a small village near Kilcoo and killed many of the poor villagers.

John de Courcy, the de facto ruler of East Ulster, had led a party of his men out from their base at Dundrum Castle to assess the situation and do what they could to seek out those responsible.

His wife, Affreca de Courcy, had insisted on accompanying him to inspect the damage and she was shocked by the wanton destruction and loss of life.

By the side of some still smouldering remains of wooden and earthen huts she spotted a young red-headed boy comforting a crying younger red-haired girl.

Lady Affreca rode over on her palfrey and then she got down from her horse and spoke to the boy, "What has happened here and why is this young girl crying so?"

"My sister is crying because our mother and father were both killed in the fighting, and I don't know what I am going to do to look after her" bravely said the young boy.

"We shall see what can be done. What are your names?"

"I am Ruaidri and this is my little sister Aoife."

"Well I am my Lord John's wife and I shall ask him if I can take you both back with us to our castle in Dundrum. Tell your sister to stop crying and also tell her that from now on I will be taking care of you both. Now follow me."

So Ruaidri turned to his sister and pulled her to her feet and told her to quieten down and they set off after the nice woman.

Lady Affreca went up to her husband and gently but firmly asked him for permission to take the two children back home with them.

John de Courcy seemed slightly irritated and bemused by the request, but looking at his little wife with genuine affection swiftly acquiesced to her demands.

So they set off and left the ruined village behind.

Chapter 2 – 1198

When they arrived at Dundrum the children were awed by the size of the castle rising up in front of them. They had never even seen a castle before and the stone walls seemed to stretch up so high.

They came in through the gateway and entered the large courtyard of Dundrum Castle situated on top of a rocky hilltop.

It was one of John de Courcy's two major fortified strongholds, the other being Carrickfergus Castle further North.

Servants and attendants came rushing to help the Lord and Lady dismount and see to their horses. The children were swept up by Affreca like a mother hen and ushered inside the great hall.

And over the next few weeks, under the kind and watchful eyes of the Lady Affreca, the two children started to settle in and get used to the castle buildings and its grassy surroundings.

The boy was slight of stature and sometimes seemed a bit timid and unsure of his circumstances, not unnaturally with the recent dreadful loss of his parents.

However the younger girl soon became not so quiet and was always running around laughing and giggling and occasionally getting in the way of the great Lord himself.

Initially John de Courcy looked at her thunderously from under his brows, but then couldn't refrain from smiling at her antics as she warmed his heart with her bright happy ways.

Aoife had made a conquest of both the lord and his sweet, childless lady.

19

Shortly thereafter Lady Affreca made a decision to change their names to the Anglo-Norman way of spelling and for them to now be called Rory and Eva.

The newly renamed Rory was not sure he really liked or appreciated the change but went along with it anyway.

Rory showed some liking and aptitude for making music and started to learn to play the traditional Irish harp.

He was taught by a grizzled old man with a long white beard called Brogan, who seemed somewhat severe but was actually quite understanding in putting up with Rory's initially fumbling attempts at playing.

The old man always said there's no point shouting and ranting to try and get someone to learn; you're always better off encouraging and praising effort made.

Gently Brogan cajoled Rory until his playing picked up and gradually improved.

The boy Rory was also lucky in being taught some of how to read and write by the local monks at the Lady Affreca's insistence.

Time passed and Rory and Eva were able to slowly forget about the very worst of the past and grow into being part of the inhabitants of the castle community.

It is sometimes remarkable how resilient the young can be in the face of adversity.

Chapter 3 – 1199

Often John de Courcy and his armed retainers would go out on patrols and also head off North to Downpatrick and then sometimes onto Carrickfergus Castle.

And after one of these trips Lord John came back in a towering rage, and could be heard talking in a very loud voice in the great hall to the Lady Affreca.

"Is it not bad enough that John is now king and I knew he liked me not – but now I hear that he has actually authorised that young upstart Hugh de Lacy to wage war on me and bring me down!"

"I have used much of my power for good these last few years, or at least better than those dogs would use the people of Ulster if they ruled over them."

"Calm, husband, maybe you could think of a way to try and appease the king?"

"No, that man is nasty, devious and vindictive and I wonder how England and Ireland will fare with him in power."

"You knew well the young man's old father; is there no peace you can broker with the younger Hugh de Lacy?"

"If only I could, but this fawning toady seeks to be a favourite of the king by his bootlicking and grovelling."

"Well, by God, let them try to overthrow me! I have been here a score of years and more building up my castles and defences and I won't let my lands be taken away from me without a fight!"

"Well said, I am sure you will give a good account of yourself" reassuringly said Affreca.

"Yes, and just as long as you are kept safe too, my dear" said John de Courcy with heartfelt concern and affection for his wife.

"If right is might then as we are in the right so verily God shall make us mighty!"

Unfortunately fanciful illusions often become the delusory dreams by which some men wish to live.

Chapter 4 – 1200 to 1203

Over the next couple of years many attacks were made on John de Courcy and his lands, and gradually his enemies were chipping away at his carefully constructed chain of defences and accustomed way of life.

But although his power was weakened somewhat still he was not anywhere near broken or completely beaten yet.

In early 1203 a sturdy man-at-arms came over from Wales to join up with his forces. He was a seasoned veteran of the wars in France and had recently left Brittany after the defeat and capture of his former liege lord the young Prince Arthur, Duke of Brittany.

Now that he had heard that the teenager Prince had disappeared and been secretly disposed of on the orders of King John, he was determined to fight for any who stood up against the power of this false and murderous king.

By the Bretons he had apparently become known as David Le Grishomme seemingly because his short, unruly hair was all peppery grey; or maybe because he had no device on his plain shield.

Although he seemed quite blunt and dour to start with, in matter of fact Rory got to like his quiet manner and sensible conversation. Still he seemed to have some secrets locked away in his past.

Brogan the old harper took ill and sickened; Rory and David tried their best to make him feel more comfortable and the soldier gave the elderly man some whiskey to dull the pain.

Brogan turned slowly to David Le Grishomme and weakly said

"That boy's a good harper in the making, but he ain't no soldier though, will you promise to keep him safe?"

"I cannot say so for certes, but I will promise to keep an eye out for him and I always stick to my word when given whatever the cost."

"Well thankee for that then" coughed the frail old man.

And overnight in the dark and the howling wind and rain Brogan died and most sadly they buried him the next day.

He left instructions for his best harp to be given to Rory for him to use from now on.

Chapter 5 – 1204

Hugh de Lacy was becoming concerned that King John might be getting impatient and unhappy with the time being taken to oust John de Courcy from Ulster.

So he redoubled his efforts to find a way and paid out bribes to suborn several of de Courcy's own men and induce them to pass over information.

De Lacy questioned them about how he might capture their former lord and it also came to be mentioned that John de Courcy had a known reputation as a very pious, God-fearing man.

And these turncoats said it was simply not possible to easily ambush him since he always remained in his armour and kept a group of bodyguards close to hand.

Except on one day of the year when on Good Friday it was his usual longstanding custom to wear no armour and carry no shield nor weapon, but simply attend church with his wife piously kneeling at his prayers after he had gone around the church five times bare-footed. So a plot was set in place and they waited expectantly for Easter to come round.

Hugh de Lacy and a band of his soldiers stealthily moved into concealed positions around that church on Good Friday 1204 and waited for de Courcy to enter the building and then they sprung the trap and burst in upon him.

John de Courcy was startled and caught completely unawares but was such a formidable warrior that he took them all on alone by grabbing the wooden cross pole and wielding it about him most ferociously.

He defended himself until it was broken and it was said he slew at least a dozen opponents before he was finally dragged down and captured.

John de Courcy was tied up and brought before a triumphant Hugh de Lacy who told him that King John had ordered him banished from Ireland in just the clothes he stood in and without his wife or any other possessions.

He was to be forthwith taken to the nearest harbour where he was to be put on a boat to sail away into exile as an outcast and traitor.

As de Courcy was led away the rest of the stunned congregation was ushered out of the church.

The Lady Affreca and Eva were to be sent to the nearby Grey Abbey monastery, that she had herself endowed and founded, to be looked after there.

Rory just stood there in shock wondering what was going to happen next.

Chapter 6 – 1204

The first thing John de Courcy's soldiers knew about all this was when Hugh de Lacy's armed men suddenly came up into Dundrum Castle and took it over.

Caught unawares there was nothing further they could do and Hugh de Lacy offered them the choice of further paid employment under him or an uncertain lordless future outside – most men naturally accepted and now pledged their allegiance to him.

Early on David Le Grishomme managed to slip out past the guards and headed down to the church to find Rory and learn what had happened.

He was shocked to hear of the complete success of the ambush and the obvious scale of its planning and execution.

They both agreed that they wanted to see what they could do to help out, and David said he had given his solemn oath to John de Courcy as his liege lord and so felt honour bound not to break his word.

So they devised a rough plan and went into the deserted church to borrow some robes and vestments to enable them to dress up as a priest and a young clerk.

Then they went down to the nearby harbour and hurried to get onto the boat that John de Courcy was being held on, awaiting the turning of the tide.

Posing as a priest David was able to invoke dire warnings of eternal damnation and using his own money managed to bribe the guards and boat captain to give them passage to the Isle of Man and there to hand John de Courcy over to the care of his wife's relatives.

Hence they sailed over to the Isle of Man and John de Courcy was released onto that island.

He immediately started to make preparations to get an invasion force together with the aid of his brother-in-law Ragnvald Godredsson to return to Ulster and retake his possessions.

Chapter 7 – 1205

As time dragged on, in May 1205 King John made Hugh de Lacy the Earl of Ulster, granting him all the lands of the province "as John de Courcy held it on the day when Hugh defeated him."

It was a difficult time for Rory and David being cooped up on the Isle of Man, but then John de Courcy's fleet was ready and they sailed back across the Irish Sea in July 1205 with Norse soldiers and a hundred longships supplied by his brother-in-law Ragnvald.

They sailed into Dundrum Bay and landed. Their forces quickly encircled the castle and preparations were made to assault the walls.

Led by John de Courcy the Norsemen attacked; but the walls were so thick and the defences so strong that they were repulsed with heavy losses.

They tried once more but again without success. It certainly did seem like the castle fortifications John de Courcy had constructed were so well-built that they might not be breached or scaled at all easily.

Ragnvald said to his brother-in-law "I fear you have made the castle too strong to be taken."

"We will try again tomorrow" grimly said de Courcy.

The next day John de Courcy sent David and Rory over to Grey Abbey monastery to pass a message onto Lady Affreca.

"Your husband says he will come to fetch you as soon as he has taken the castle."

"Then let us hope that things go well and he will come quickly" replied the Lady Affreca as she tried to raise the flicker of a smile. But it was a sad smile all the same.

Rory gave a rushed goodbye to his sister Eva, who as a near teenager was looking slightly bored at her confinement there.

David and Rory were riding back towards the castle when they spotted in the distance a large band of men moving swiftly towards Dundrum.

They wondered who these men might be, then realised with grim shock that they carried the banners of Walter de Lacy, Hugh's elder brother.

This enemy force moved forward into the attack and caught de Courcy's men completely by surprise and unprepared.

Walter de Lacy's men cleaved through the ranks of the Norsemen and the panic turned into a rout as they streamed away from the castle walls.

As John de Courcy was trying to organise a fightback he was overwhelmed in the melee of battle and captured.

Ragnvald Godredsson saw that the battle was lost and shouted to his defeated men to run. "To the boats! Back to the boats!"

And a general pandemonium ensued as his men broke and ran back towards Dundrum Bay where the longships had been anchored.

Many men were killed in the panicked retreat as what remained of the host scrambled into the boats and sailed away.

Rory and David managed to ride down to the seashore and escape in one of the longships and looked back on a scene of death and devastation.

And up there on top of the rocky hilltop they could just make out John de Courcy being led away into Dundrum Castle for whatever punishment might await him.

PART TWO
1205 – 1214

Chapter 8 – 1205 to 1206

By a series of journeys they made for Wales where David Le Grishomme said he would hopefully have some contacts from the distant past long ago.

They had heard that King John had John de Courcy swiftly imprisoned in a dark and horrible dungeon under the control of Hugh de Lacy's oversight.

Having been dropped off on the Isle of Anglesey in autumn 1205, David and Rory passed quickly through the town of Conwy as its lord, Prince Llywelyn, was presently closely allied and connected with King John having just recently got married to John's young daughter Joan (by one of his former mistresses).

So they headed eastwards into North East Wales to the principality of Powys Fadog ruled by Madog ap Gruffudd.

He was currently involved in conflict caught between the forces of Prince Llywelyn of Gwynedd and the English Marcher Lords including the important William de Braose.

And so Prince Madog was happy to take on such an experienced fighter as David Le Grishomme; and David managed to persuade the prince to accept Rory as some sort of retainer and also as a harper to play music to the soldiers.

It seemed that David was slightly known of by some of the older Welsh warriors who sometimes whispered as he went by.

Gradually Rory heard words spoken that David was somehow connected to an old English family over in Cheshire from a village called Malpas near the large town of Chester.

David grudgingly admitted that he was born not far away but then clammed up and didn't go into any further details.

There appeared to be some deeper, dark reason why he seemed unhappy to talk about the secrets of his past.

The warband of Powys Fadog was kept busy and there were various skirmishes and the impetus ebbed and flowed backwards and forwards both ways over time.

Horses went lame; people got sick; men died; wives and mothers lamented and grieved. It was often cold and wet and they ran short of food.

Many times at night Rory would take his harp out of its bag – Brogan's faithful old harp – and play music and songs to entertain the Welsh soldiers around the campfires where they sat and huddled after their meagre evening meals.

Chapter 9 – 1206

One day in late autumn 1206 most of Powys' forces had left the main camp early to head South to attack the lands of some Marcher Lord or other.

Later a group of riders appeared on the horizon – everyone looked in their direction and stared hard to try and see who they were.

Suddenly they spurred their horses and burst into the camp putting to the sword the few guards and killing a number of the cooks and camp followers and some of the serving boys.

Whilst they raided the stores and grabbed what they could, their leader reined in his horse near Rory and seeing his harp bag demanded the thin young man to play a tune for him.

Rory bristled and stuck out his chin and refused "No, I will not play for you. You are a foul murderer for killing defenceless boys and women!"

The man jumped down from his horse and angrily said "I like to think of myself as a bit of a rough diamond, but some of my men may call me worse than that. Play for me, boy, or I'll have you whipped!"

"Go on, Rory, you'd best play something for him" piped up one of the other servants.

"I will not" defiantly answered back Rory.

"Then maybe if I cut off a couple of your fingers you'll never play the harp again, you little Irish whelp" evilly hissed the enemy chief.

Just then the sound of a hunting horn was heard and one of the raiders came up to say a band of Welsh foot soldiers and horsemen was heading their way fast and that they had better leave.

The leader strode back to his horse and mounted up; wheeling round he turned to Rory and gave him a sour look "Well, I mark your name, young Rory, and I can wait till another time. My name is Nigel de Malpas and I will have my revenge on you!"

And he harshly spurred his horse and he and his men rode off in the opposite direction to the hurriedly returning Welshmen.

All that had happened was told to Prince Madog, who cursed at the ease with which the camp had been raided and vital supplies stolen and people killed.

Surely they must have had some knowledge that their warband was going out raiding far afield that day?

And the name of Nigel de Malpas as the leader was mentioned and at that Rory noticed David Le Grishomme shuddered and went pale.

Later on that evening, when sat down together, Rory told David all about his run-in with Nigel de Malpas and wondered if David could tell him anything more about the man.

David looked at Rory with a hard stare and then shrugged his shoulders and sighed deeply.

"Oh yes, I know a lot about that nasty piece of work. A vicious, vile and treacherous creature who betrayed me and my family, and probably also my young prince over in Brittany as well."

"He is a sort of cousin to me. His father was my father's elder brother but there was some trouble over my mother; and when my father died Nigel and his father threw my mother off our lands. Apparently the cur even tried to lay his dirty hands on her! Penniless and bereft, not long after she died."

"I was many hundreds of miles away soldiering in France – not knowing anything!"

"Then many years later Nigel and I somehow ended up in Brittany apparently both fighting for young Prince Arthur, so I had to accept his presence. He always looked at me strangely and I hated being around him - and I felt sure that he was untrustworthy and I believe he was a traitor and gave information to King John's forces allowing us to be surprised and defeated in battle."

"Anyway he disappeared and only much later on did I find out the true facts of what had happened about my mother. I have always been on the move since then and never seen him again face-to-face. And when I do I will try to kill him for all the wrongs he has done!"

"You'd best steer well clear of him if you want to stay alive!"

And with that David le Grishomme stiffly stood up and walked unsteadily away from Rory and the campfire.

Rory just sat there in dismay and confusion.

Chapter 10 – 1207 to 1208

At the height of his power and influence and with granted lands in England, Wales and Ireland the prominent lord William de Braose fell out of favour with King John.

The arbitrary and fickle nature of royal favouritism was fully exposed by the king's dangerous spitefulness and cruelty.

The precise reasons remain uncertain and obscure but his fall was sudden and the king's anger and vindictiveness was harsh and severe.

King John had much rewarded William de Braose for keeping quiet around the time of the disappearance of Prince Arthur of Brittany and perhaps he felt threatened by the knowledge William had.

Furthermore King John made some mention of overdue monies that de Braose may have owed the Crown Treasury from his estates, but the king's actions went way beyond what was required to recover any debts.

He seized William de Braose's English lands in Sussex and Devon and also sent a military force into Wales to grab all his estates there.

Now on the run and harried on all sides Lord William felt compelled to seek alliance with Prince Madog of Powys Fadog.

For sure he did not have an unblemished reputation as a Marcher Lord in his dealings with the Welsh and having fought with them, but he was still a powerful baron with men and resources to call upon and Prince Madog judged he could be useful in more upcoming conflict.

David Le Grishomme was not happy with the situation, as he knew William de Braose had been involved in the original capturing of Prince Arthur, but as a mere lowly soldier he had to go along with the wishes of his current lord.

Prince Madog mounted some military actions along with the forces of William de Braose and they managed to keep King John at bay.

In 1208 Prince Gwenwynwyn ap Owain of the Southern province of Powys Wenwynwyn also fell out with the English king, who summoned him to Shrewsbury in October 1208 and then foully arrested him.

Prince Llywelyn took the opportunity to annex Southern Powys and was now firmly in the ascendancy in Wales.

And greater pressure fell on William de Braose as one by one his castles were assailed and captured. It was taking time but gradually he was running out of men, money and support.

Chapter 11 – 1208 to 1209

William de Braose was forced to flee out of Wales over to Ireland, somewhat reluctantly accompanied by David Le Grishomme and Rory, who at least knew the country and the make-up of the many alliances between the Irish clans.

Steering clear of the main Anglo-Norman towns they took a nomadic journey between the various Irish provinces.

And although previously a very powerful lord now William de Braose was a much diminished figure, viewed not as a potential asset to any alliance but more as a hindrance or obstacle in dealing with the difficult agents of King John.

But then things got worse as King John issued orders for de Braose to be hunted down in Ireland, and he further ordered Hugh de Lacy to actively set out to capture him.

The Earl of Ulster sent messengers to the various provincial royal courts demanding that the Irish kings have no more dealings with the fugitive and hand him over.

Always moving on, a couple of times they had to pack up quickly and leave camps not long before groups of armed soldiers would have intercepted them.

Eventually things became so difficult that they just had to leave Ireland and seek ship to return back over to Wales.

On the boat David Le Grishomme finally faced up to William de Braose and asked him about his involvement in the disappearance of Prince Arthur.

Lord William looked down sorrowfully and slumped slightly as he drew breath and then slowly spoke.

"I knew King John was a cruel and nasty man, and yet as he was king I went along with many bad things that happened and I gained lands and favours from him."

"But even I did not believe how low he could stoop. Yes, we captured Prince Arthur after that shambolic battle at Mirebeau and he was transferred to Rouen under my charge for a short time."

"Next I was sent away to rejoin the army in campaigning against the French king. And then suddenly I heard he had disappeared – and I knew that the vile man must have had his own nephew killed. Which I was never a party to, you must believe me."

"He was an innocent young man and surely would have been a better king than this evil tyrant we have now" said David.

"They say that he who sups with the devil should keep his distance or he will mix with death. I am sorry for many of the things I have done, but for my involvement in his loss most of all."

And with that William de Braose walked away towards the bow of the ship lost deeply in his own sad and bitter thoughts.

Chapter 12 – 1210 to 1211

In 1210 the good relationship between Prince Llywelyn and King John fractured and deteriorated and led to all out rebellion and war.

Llywelyn forged an alliance with William de Braose which seemed to please the old man and rejuvenated his fighting spirit.

An army led by Earl Ranulph of Chester invaded the lands of Gwynedd. Prince Llywelyn destroyed his own castle at Deganwy to bar its use by the English and retreated West of the River Conwy.

The Earl of Chester quickly rebuilt Deganwy, and then Llywelyn retaliated by attacking and ravaging the earl's lands.

And matters got worse when King John released Prince Gwenwynwyn from captivity, and sent soldiers to help him retake Southern Powys Wenwynwyn back off Prince Llywelyn.

Then came most exceedingly terrible news for William de Braose. His longstanding wife Maud had also incurred the deep enmity of King John.

Previously as part of the disgrace and fall of the house of de Braose, King John had demanded that William and Maud's eldest son, named William also, be sent to him as a hostage.

Maud had refused and apparently stated too loudly within earshot of the king's officers that "she would not deliver her children to a king who had murdered his own nephew." When reported, this further incensed King John.

Maud and her eldest son had to flee and went over to Ireland, but eventually they were captured and sent back to England later in 1210.

Maud and younger William de Braose were firstly imprisoned at the royal Windsor Castle, but were then afterwards transferred further away to Corfe Castle in Dorset and placed in a deep, dark dungeon.

And there they were both most horribly starved to death.

Supposedly the evil King John ordered that a sheaf of oats and one piece of raw bacon be given to them, and they then just be ignored and left down there to rot.

Finally after about eleven days the clearly dead mother and son were looked at and found lying there most piteously.

When the news was conveyed to the older William de Braose his knees buckled and he crumpled to the ground. David and Rory picked him up and even David Le Grishomme could feel some sympathy for his loss and grief.

The by now thoroughly defeated William de Braose fled Wales disguised as a beggar and went into exile in France.

Ultimately the broken old man died in August 1211 and was buried in the Abbey of St Victor in Paris by Stephen Langton, the exiled Archbishop of Canterbury and also an outspoken opponent of King John.

Chapter 13 – 1211

Early in 1211 King John invaded Gwynedd with the aid of all the other Welsh princes, planning to dispossess Llywelyn and destroy him utterly.

Unsure of who they should be supporting, David Le Grishomme and Rory managed to stay away and steer clear of any of the fighting.

The first invasion was pushed back, but later in August 1211 King John tried again with a larger army and crossed the River Conwy and poured around Snowdonia and burnt the town of Bangor.

Prince Llywelyn was forced to seek terms and on the wise advice of his council sent his wife Joan to negotiate with her father the king.

Joan was able to persuade her father not to dispossess her husband completely, but the Welsh Prince had to give up all his lands East of the River Conwy.

Also he had to pay a large tribute in cattle and horses and to hand over hostages including his illegitimate son Gruffydd.

And he was forced to agree that if he died without a legitimate heir by Joan then his lands would revert to the King of England.

The fighting had ceased and David and Rory left Powys Fadog and journeyed to the town of Conwy in Gwynedd and wondered what they would do next. Maybe they could join Prince Llywelyn now.

With access now available back into North Wales, after a few more weeks a certain Nigel de Malpas was able to also enter the town of Conwy and then set about finding out the whereabouts of Rory and his companions.

He decided that now was the time to put in place a plot to get his bloody revenge on the young Irish harper.

Chapter 14 – 1211

Nigel de Malpas entered the dirty, foul-smelling tavern and looked around scornfully; seeing all he needed to he approached these two scruffy ruffians sitting drinking ale at a rickety wooden table over in the corner.

He looked down at them with disdain "McGuinn and McGuire?"

"Who wants to know?" sneered the shorter one of them.

"I hear you are the ones to see about getting a nasty little job done round here."

"Might be. I always says dirty deeds done dirt cheap are our speciality, don't I, Billy boy?"

"Oh yes you do, and very often too" babbled the other taller man.

McGuinn cuffed McGuire about the head to shut him up.

"And where exactly did you hear about us then?"

"From the sergeant-at-arms over at Chester Castle."

"Old po-face then. Well what exactly are you wanting done?"

"Actually quite a grave thing – I want somebody inconvenient despatched to the grave and quietly put an end to."

"Now you're talking – but that'll cost you – twelve silver shillings is our price."

"I'll pay you five shillings now, and five more when the deed is done – that's my offer; take it or leave it."

"All right, all right, we'll take your price. Who's the fella?"

"He's a short young Irishman called Rory or Ruaidri and he'll be wearing a black cloak with a hood and tonight he'll be sleeping in a barn behind the Dragon tavern. Wait till he's alone and then do away with him."

"It'll be our pleasure to do your honour's bidding, so long as the money's forthcoming, don't you know."

Accordingly Nigel de Malpas handed over the first five shillings of blood money.

Later that night the two cut-throats went over to the Dragon tavern which they knew well and kept a lookout on the barn doors.

Various men went in and came out but then they saw a short man wearing a dark cloak wander over and go in.

Seeing that he was totally alone they followed him in quietly whilst pulling their daggers out of their belts.

And the next morning at their tavern roost they were confronted by a visibly angry instigator of the foul plot.

"You idiots, you've killed the wrong man!"

"And how so would that be sir, because we killed the man in the place you said."

"Yes, but I have seen that young man Rory walking about today!"

"Well the man we killed said his name was Rory or something like that when we asked him nicely like just before he died."

"You've killed a little Welshman called Rhodri Fychan!"

"So one man called Rory something or other in the right place seemed more than like enough to be your man, don't you know."

"I've a good mind not to pay you the balance."

"Oh now sir, that wouldn't be very nice of you and Billy here might not appreciate that."

"No, I wouldn't like that" grunted out McGuire looking venomous.

"Don't worry, I'll pay you to keep you quiet, but you've really messed things up for me."

"Oh could we not try again sir, for a little extra money?"

"No, damn you, he and his friends are on their guard now."

And with that Nigel de Malpas turned on his heel and walked away.

Chapter 15 – 1211 to 1212

The death of that Welshman in the barn of the tavern where he could have been sleeping last night had unnerved Rory.

David Le Grishomme knew that some English knights and soldiers were in Conwy for negotiations, and had also heard rumours that Nigel de Malpas was amongst them.

He gave Rory the news and told him that he and their companions would keep an eye on him and protect him; but he could see that Rory was frightened and scared by this turn of events.

David wondered to himself what would happen if he ever met up again with that snake Nigel de Malpas, and would he be able to get his revenge for all the terrible hurt done to his dead mother?

Later that evening when they were sitting alone by the campfire out in a clearing near the edge of town, they suddenly heard the noise of someone approaching through the trees.

A man called out from the dark and said "I'm coming in."

And Nigel de Malpas walked forward into the firelight.

"So finally we meet again after all this time, you uncommon rogue, David."

"By God, you are a scurvy rat and always will be. I have not forgotten how you abandoned and betrayed Prince Arthur over in Brittany."

"How so, cousin, I just deserted a sinking ship. King John was obviously going to win, so I left and joined up with him."

David carried on "Remember how I said we should post more guards around the perimeter of the camp before we were caught unawares and surprised."

49

"Yes you did, but nobody listened. Arthur was young and foolish and his advisers were incompetent idiots. Not my fault."

"Well the young man did not deserve to die."

"He lost, that is all."

"You are a disgrace to our ancestors and family name."

"Come to that, at least I am a truly direct descendant!"

"My dear mother was lied to about the plans for a wedding. And you and your father threw her out and left her destitute to die!"

"Unlucky then, eh?" sneered Nigel. "Anyway enough of this reminiscing, I have come for retribution against this young whelp for all his meddling against the wishes of King John. Stand out of the way."

"I will do no such thing; you will have to fight me first before you get to him."

"Then so be it, I shall kill you too – and with great pleasure."

Rory looked on with fear in his eyes as the two older men drew their swords and faced up to each other with deadly intent.

They circled round probing each other and then Nigel de Malpas leapt forward and thrust at David. They slashed and parried and their sharp, deadly blades rang out as they clashed.

Then a sudden lunge by Nigel took David unawares and he was wounded and then he was caught by a backhanded slash from Nigel.

Things were going badly and David's sword arm was bleeding heavily and he was finding it harder to parry the increasingly deadly blows of the advancing Nigel.

Blowing hard and in obvious great pain David staggered and Nigel de Malpas went in for the kill with evident triumph gleaming in his eyes.

Desperately David appeared to almost run onto Nigel's sword but yet with his own sword outstretched he managed to skewer the evil man right through.

"Die you faithless spawn of the devil!"

They both fell heavily to the ground and Nigel de Malpas' lifeless eyes looked up in empty astonishment.

David Le Grishomme was just barely alive and Rory rushed over to him and cradled his shattered and bloody body.

"Well at least we are both free of him now" hoarsely whispered the brave grey-haired friend of his. Rory looked on distraught.

"You'd be wise to go back home to Ireland soon and try to steer clear of any of King John's men. Live well, my good young friend" and with that then he shuddered and died.

Rory knelt there and wiped away at his bitterly flowing tears.

Thereafter elseways Prince Llywelyn recovered his fortunes quickly.

The other Welsh princes who had supported King John soon became disillusioned with his autocratic rule and lack of understanding and changed sides again.

They even had the spiritual and temporal support of the Pope who was now also in a long-running dispute with King John.

Llywelyn was able to recover almost all of Gwynedd that he had previously lost in just a few months of 1212.

Rory felt now was the right time for him to return to Ireland and he took his leave of the prince and sailed over to Strangford Lough.

Chapter 16 – 1213

Disembarking, Rory found shelter back at the nearby monastery of Grey Abbey which Lady Affreca had all those years ago originally founded.

Several nights later a monk came to get him saying that there was a fine lady here asking to see him.

Rory went to the dining hall and there sitting on a bench at one of the wooden trestle tables was a beautiful young red-haired woman richly attired in a fine dress and with an expensive looking cloak.

Recognition slowly dawned on Rory "Aoife is it you?"

"Yes, Rory, it is I; and I am known here as the Lady Eva."

"What are you doing here?"

"I heard tell that you were back in Ulster, and I've come to see you and find out how you are after all these many years away."

"Aye, it's been a long time and I've seen quite a few things in those years but at least I've still survived. How are things going here?"

"The Lady Affreca is living closeted in a nunnery nearby and poor old Lord John is still in prison."

"Oh dear. How are you keeping, sister?"

"I am fine and have taken measures to see that I am well looked after."

"What exactly do you mean?"

"Well after the Lady Affreca went into the nunnery, I had to decide what to do and I didn't fancy being locked up within any cold stone cloisters."

Eva looked at Rory with a firm and steady gaze "Meanwhile I had caught the eye of a high Lord and decided to try my luck with allowing him to look after me."

"Oh I see, or do I?"

"I am being well looked after by Hugh de Lacy and his power and prestige give my position some security and status. I have a house and furnishings, and sufficient money to buy fine food and have a good life."

"Then I cannot say that I blame you. I have learnt that sometimes you have to do whatever you need to manage to survive."

"I am glad you are happy for me. Being the mistress of a great lord is not always straightforward or easy. Is there anything I can do to help you?"

"I guess I will have to be moving on if people know that I am back. I was on the wrong side in the fighting of the past round here."

"No, I will put a good word in for you and smooth the problems of the past so that you should be able to stay."

"Thank you. I am not sure what I might plan to do next. I don't quite know how I would employ my skills as a harper anymore. Maybe I will have to find something else where I can use my knowledge of reading and writing."

"Perhaps I can help you get a job as a steward at one of my Lord's estates."

"That would be very kind and I would be much beholden to you."

"Stay here for a little while longer and I will see what I can do and get back to you with further news."

And they embraced and parted with rekindled love and affection.

Some weeks later the offer to be Steward down at Dundrum Castle itself was presented by a messenger from the Earl of Ulster and Rory gratefully accepted the post.

Chapter 17 – 1214

The way of life had changed for lots of the poorer peasants of Ireland, away from the herding of livestock and a rural economy over to the imposition of the feudal system tying people to the land and its lords and manors.

Gradually Rory settled into his new life handling all aspects of the administration of the running of Dundrum Castle.

Often Hugh de Lacy came to visit the castle, sometimes also accompanied by his sister Eva. There was no residual animosity between the Earl and Rory, and the past was left in the past.

Rory learnt that poor John de Courcy was languishing sick and ill in the cold, wet dungeons of Carrickfergus Castle.

In due course he enquired of Eva if there was any way that the broken old man could ever possibly be released from prison.

Eva replied that she would look into what could be done, but said she would have to tread very carefully in how to raise it with the Earl of Ulster as any action would have to be authorised by the king.

Eventually Eva came back to Rory with the tidings that she had an idea which she thought she could put to Lord Hugh to try and get approved.

She suggested that somehow they should arrange to have John de Courcy announce that he would seek to "take the Cross" and then maybe prepare later to go on a pilgrimage to the Holy Land.

Rory was most enthusiastic about her clever plan.

Finally Eva came back to say that Hugh de Lacy had been given permission to allow the aged John de Courcy released into the care of the monks of an Abbey monastery near Craigavon.

As he headed back to more of his duties in the castle, Rory was pleased and thankful that finally the grand old man would have some peace and rest.

Epilogue

John de Courcy spent the rest of his life in poverty and obscurity, but at least when he died in 1219 it was not in a horrible dungeon.

The vile and despotic King John further upset the barons and caused them to join together and revolt against him. He was forced to sign up to the provisions of Magna Carta in 1215 at Runnymede; but then reneged on his promises to keep to them and so was drawn into a civil war called the First Barons' War that lasted even after his own death from dysentery in October 1216.

He was surely one of the worst kings ever to rule England.

Hugh de Lacy, the 1st Earl of Ulster, had many fallings in and out with King John and then his young son and successor King Henry III. He wielded great power and influence in Ireland for a long time and eventually died in 1242.

Lady Eva continued to live for many years as the esteemed mistress of Hugh de Lacy.

Rory lived to a grand old age in a position of trust and security, whilst still playing his harp every now and again for his own enjoyment and pleasure.

ALSO BY THIS AUTHOR...

FOR HONOUR AND NOT FOR GLORY

A young Briton, Drustan gets caught up in conflict in Britain including the AD43 Roman Invasion and ultimately the savage AD60/61 Revolt of Queen Boudica.

He encounters challenges to his honour but will not be defeated and throughout adversity he will continue to fight "For Honour And Not For Glory".

This short novelette offers up an exciting story linked to the legend of the Hallaton Helmet and hoard discovered in Leicestershire in 2000, now on display at the Market Harborough Museum.

£5.99   ISBN: 978-0-9567753-4-4

ALSO BY THIS AUTHOR...

ALL SINS MUST BE PAID FOR

Archaeologists working on the route of the
Weymouth Relief Road in Dorset in 2008/2009
discovered a burial pit on Ridgeway Hill containing
what turned out to be 54 dismembered skeletons
and 51 skulls of Vikings executed by local Saxons.

This novelette seeks to offer a plausible tale of
what could have happened at a time of great conflict
in England between the Saxons under King Aethelred
the Unready and the Danes led by Sweyn Forkbeard
around the years AD 1002 to 1014.

It is told through the actions of Rolf, an innocent
young boy who stows away on a longship heading
across to England. But as the story unfolds, Rolf is
drawn into a maelstrom of violence and death, and
a burning need for revenge that is so all consuming
that it changes him forever. And sometimes a man
has to pay a heavy price to atone for all his misdeeds.
But is there still a chance for redemption?

£5.99   ISBN: 978-0-9567753-5-1

ALSO BY THIS AUTHOR...

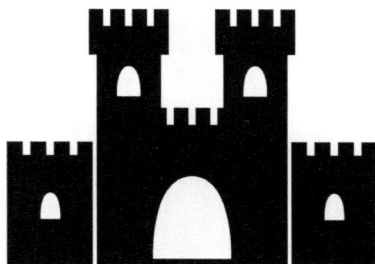

CAST NO SHADOW

Marguerite is a young girl who tragically loses all her family in rebellion and fighting in the Duchy of Gascony in France. Coming over to England in 1252 she becomes known as Margot and gets caught up in fractious strife between the barons and the king.

Along with the swordsman Jean de Savignac and the young pickpocket Tom Buckle, Margot is drawn into a web of intrigue as she plots to get the ultimate revenge she craves for. Whilst barely known to history as Margot the Spy, this spirited and quick-witted young woman has a crucial role to play in the unfolding of the dramatic action of the time.

This short novelette offers up an exciting historical story linked to the personality of Simon de Montfort and events leading up to the Second Barons' War with King Henry III and his son Prince Edward culminating in the decisive Battle of Evesham in 1265.

£5.99   ISBN: 978-0-9567753-6-8

David's 30 Favourite Rock & Pop Albums

1964	(01)	The Beatles	A Hard Day's Night
1976	(02)	Be-Bop Deluxe	Sunburst Finish
1971	(03)	Caravan	In The Land Of Grey And Pink
1979	(04)	Ry Cooder	Bop Till You Drop
1991	(05)	Crowded House	Woodface
1972	(06)	Deep Purple	Machine Head
1978	(07)	Dire Straits	Dire Straits
1975	(08)	Eagles	One Of These Nights
1977	(09)	Fleetwood Mac	Rumours
1970	(10)	Free	Fire And Water
1973	(11)	Rory Gallagher	Tattoo
1973	(12)	Genesis	Selling England By The Pound
1968	(13)	Jimi Hendrix	Electric Ladyland
1971	(14)	Led Zeppelin	IV (Four Symbols)
1974	(15)	Little Feat	Feats Don't Fail Me Now
1973	(16)	Lynyrd Skynyrd	Pronounced Leh-nerd Skin-nerd
1973	(17)	Pink Floyd	Dark Side Of The Moon
1975	(18)	Pink Floyd	Wish You Were Here
1972	(19)	Steely Dan	Can't Buy A Thrill
1976	(20)	Steely Dan	The Royal Scam
1976	(21)	Al Stewart	Year Of The Cat
1971	(22)	Rod Stewart	Every Picture Tells A Story
1975	(23)	10CC	How Dare You!
1971	(24)	James Taylor	Mud Slide Slim And The Blue Horizon
1994	(25)	Martin Taylor	Spirit Of Django
2005	(26)	Thunder	The Magnificent Seventh
2001	(27)	Peter White	Glow
1971	(28)	The Who	Who's Next
1972	(29)	Wishbone Ash	Argus
1986	(30)	XTC	Skylarking

David's 20 Favourite Guitarists from his Youth

b.1910	DJANGO REINHARDT	Gypsy Jazz Guitarist
b.1933	JULIAN BREAM	Classical Guitarist and Lutenist
b.1942	JIMI HENDRIX	of JIMI HENDRIX EXPERIENCE
b.1944	JIMMY PAGE	of LED ZEPPELIN
b.1945	RITCHIE BLACKMORE	of DEEP PURPLE and RAINBOW
b.1945	DANNY GATTON	Rockabilly and Redneck Jazz
b.1946	PETER GREEN	of original FLEETWOOD MAC
b.1948	RORY GALLAGHER	Irish Blues Rock Guitarist
b.1948	BILL NELSON	of BE-BOP DELUXE
b.1949	ANDREW LATIMER	of CAMEL
b.1950	ANDY POWELL	of WISHBONE ASH
b.1950	TED TURNER	of WISHBONE ASH
b.1950	PAUL KOSSOFF	of FREE
b.1951	PETER HAYCOCK	of CLIMAX BLUES BAND
b.1951	WALTER TROUT	Blues Rock Guitarist
b.1951	ROBBEN FORD	Blues, Jazz and Rock Guitarist
b.1952	GARY MOORE	Rock and Blues Guitarist
b.1953	LAURIE WISEFIELD	of WISHBONE ASH
b.1954	STEVIE RAY VAUGHAN	"SRV" Blues Rock Guitarist
b.1956	MARTIN TAYLOR	Jazz and Solo Guitarist